Enid Blyton's ENCHANTED WORLD

Bizzy and the Bedtime Bear

By Elise Allen

EGMONT

Meet the
Faraway Fairies

Favourite Colour — Yellow. It's a beautiful colour that reminds me of sunshine and happiness.

Talent — Light. I can release rays of energy to light up a room or, if I really try hard, I can use it to break out of tight situations. The only problem is that when I lose my temper I can have a 'flash attack' which is really embarrassing because my friends find it funny.

Favourite Activity — Exploring. I love an adventure, even when it gets me into trouble. I never get tired of visiting new places and meeting new people.

Favourite Colour — Blue. The colour of the sea and the sky. I love every shade from aquamarine to midnight blue.

Talent — As well as being a musician I can also transform into other objects. I like to do it for fun, but it also comes in useful if there's a spot of bother.

Favourite Activity — Singing and dancing. I can do it all day and never get tired.

Silky the Fairy enters the Land of Mine-All-Mine from the Faraway Tree looking for adventure. She has visited many Lands in search of fun and excitement. But when she meets Talon the evil Troll she soon finds that her Enchanted World is turned upside down.

To rescue the Talismans that have been lost from the Faraway Tree, Silky will need some help, and fast! Luckily she can rely on her best fairy friends to help her in her task. With the special talents of Melody, Petal, Pinx and Bizzy, Silky must save the Lands of the Enchanted World. But will the fairies succeed or will Talon get his evil way?

EGMONT

We bring stories to life

Bizzy and the Bedtime Bear
Published in Great Britain 2009
by Egmont UK Limited
239 Kensington High Street, London W8 6SA

Text and illustrations
ENID BLYTON® ENID BLYTON'S ENCHANTED
WORLD™ Copyright © 2009 Chorion Rights Limited.
All rights reserved.

Text by Elise Allen
Illustrations by Dynamo

ISBN 978 1 4052 4569 2

1 3 5 7 9 10 8 6 4 2

A CIP catalogue record for this title is available from the British
Library

Printed and bound in Great Britain by the CPI Group

Favourite Colour – Green. It's the colour of life. All my best plant friends are one shade of green or another.

Talent – I can speak to the animals and plants of the Enchanted World ... not to mention the ones in the Faraway Tree.

Favourite Activity – I love to sit peacefully and listen to the constant chatter of all creatures, both big and small.

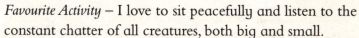

Favourite Colour – Pink. What other colour would it be? Pink is simply the best colour there is.

Talent – Apart from being a supreme fashion designer, I can also become invisible. It helps me to escape from my screaming fashion fans!

Favourite Activity – Designing. Give me some fabrics and I'll make you something fabulous. Remember – If it's not by Pinx ... your makeover stinks!

Favourite Colour – Orange. It's the most fun colour of all. It's just bursting with life!

Talent – Being a magician of course. Although I have been known to make the odd Basic Bizzy Blunder with my spells.

Favourite Activity – Baking Brilliant Blueberry Buns and Marvellous Magical Muffins. There is always time to bake a tasty cake to show your friends that you care.

www.blyton.com/enchantedworld

Contents

Introduction

*T*ucked away among the thickets, groves and
forests of our Earth is a special wood. An
Enchanted Wood, where the trees grow taller, the
branches grow stronger and the leaves grow denser
than anywhere else. Search hard enough within this
Enchanted Wood, and you'll find one tree that
towers above all the others. This is the Faraway Tree,
and it is very special. It is home to magical creatures
like elves and fairies, even a dragon. But the most
magical thing about this very magical Tree? It is the
sole doorway to the Lands of the Enchanted World.

Most of the time, the Lands of the Enchanted
World simply float along, unattached to anything.
But at one time or another, they each come to rest at

the top of the Faraway Tree. And if you're lucky enough to be in the Tree at the time, you can climb to its very top, scramble up the long Ladder extending from its tallest branch, push through the clouds and step into that Land.

Of course, there's no telling when a Land will come to the Faraway Tree, or how long it will remain. A Land might stay for months, or be gone within the hour. And if you haven't made it back down the Ladder and into the Faraway Tree before the Land floats away, you could be stuck for a very long time. This is scary even in the most wonderful of Lands, like the Land of Perfect Birthday Parties. But if you get caught in a place like the Land of Ravenous Toothy Beasts, the situation is absolutely terrifying. Yet even though exploring the Lands has its perils, it's also exhilarating, which is why creatures from all over the Enchanted World (and the occasional visiting human) come to live in the Faraway Tree so they can travel from Land to Land.

Of course, not everyone explores the Lands for

pleasure alone. In fact, five fairies have been asked do so for the ultimate cause: to save the life of the Faraway Tree and make sure the doorway to the Enchanted World remains open. These are their stories . . .

Chapter One

Panic at the Party

How had Bizzy ever let Pinx talk her into this? From her room high in the fairies' treehouse, Bizzy looked down at the crowd and gasped. Nearly every single resident of the Faraway Tree was jammed into the main room, and their excited chatter blended into a wordless, ebbing and flowing roar, like the sound of ocean waves crashing on to the beach. Bizzy felt a little seasick.

The party had originally been Bizzy's idea. It had been a few months since the fairies moved to the Faraway Tree, and Bizzy thought it would be tremendous fun to have a celebration in the treehouse. Pinx had loved the idea and taken over the organisation, transforming the fun little party into a magnificent gala of epic proportions. She had decided that Melody would be in charge of music, Silky would handle the lighting, Petal would decorate and Bizzy . . .

'You can use your magic to create the party theme!' Pinx had exclaimed.

'What do you mean?' Bizzy had asked.

'The best parties have themes,' Pinx had enthused. 'Like "Under the Sea" or "Over the Rainbow" or . . .' Pinx gasped and her eyes grew wide, '. . ."*Among the Stars*"! Yes! And with your magic you can actually make it seem as if the treehouse is in outer space! You can make shooting stars, and swirling galaxies, and . . . and no gravity! We won't just dance at this party; we'll *float*! It'll be the most incredible thing the Faraway Tree has ever seen!'

Bizzy could only gape as Pinx went on and on. Turn the treehouse into outer space? Turn off gravity? Bizzy knew that she had the magical skills to do it, but her record wasn't exactly perfect when it came to making her spells work. Bizzy was sure that one way or another, this would turn into a terrible mess.

'I don't know, Pinx,' she said. 'Maybe I could just make snacks for the party. I'm Fantastically Famous For Fantabulous Food!'

'That's a great idea!' Pinx agreed.

Bizzy relaxed . . . almost.

'So it's settled then,' Pinx continued. 'You're in charge of food and theming.'

'But –' Bizzy began to object.

'Can't talk – got to spread the word!' Pinx said, and flew off.

Between then and the party, Bizzy had tried about a million times to explain to Pinx that counting on her to turn the party into a Grand Galactic Gala was a *bad* idea. Unfortunately, Pinx seemed only to hear the words 'Grand Galactic Gala', which was how she described the party to every single creature in the Tree . . . all of whom were now inside the treehouse. They talked, they danced, they munched on Bizzy-baked delights like Crackle Corn, Gigglybeans and Goo-drops . . . but mostly, Bizzy knew, they were waiting for Bizzy to reveal her incredible theme.

Pinx soared high above everyone's heads. It was time for Bizzy's 'grand entrance' – another Pinx idea, and the reason why Bizzy was tucked away in her room. Melody stopped the music and Silky concentrated a spotlight on Pinx. Everyone looked up expectantly.

'Faraway Tree friends!' Pinx cried. 'It is now my great pleasure to present Bizzy, who will turn this party into a Grand Galactic Gala!'

'HURRAY!' cheered the crowd.

Pinx flew up to Bizzy's room and escorted her out. The crowd roared even louder when Bizzy appeared. Witch Whisper, Cluecatcher, Dame Washalot, Moonface, Saucepan Man, Elf Cloudshine, Zuni, Misty . . . even the Eternal Bloom had been moved out of her spot in Petal's garden to be part of the excitement. They were all crowded together, pressed shoulder to shoulder amidst the towering branches of the tree. Of course Bizzy's best friends were there as well – Silky, Petal, Melody and Pinx – all smiling at her, waiting for her to do exactly what Pinx had promised. Bizzy really didn't want to let them down. She took a deep breath.

'Here goes nothing,' she said to herself.

She caught Silky's eye, and Silky nodded, assuring Bizzy that it would be fine, that she could do this. Bizzy hoped that her friend was right. She raised her arms high, then spoke the spells that would turn the room into a zero-gravity fantasy land, filled with shooting stars.

'Gravitateraminous, whizzeeo-starreeo-zoomerangle-swooshlesticks!'

Bizzy plunged ten feet towards the ground. Below her, every guest dropped to the floor with a loud thump.

'What's going on?' wailed Moonface. 'I can't stand up!'

Bizzy hadn't got rid of gravity; she had made it *stronger*! Every move felt like swimming through treacle.

Then came the shooting stars. At least, they were supposed to be shooting stars, but Bizzy got the spell just a little bit mixed up and made shooting *bars*. Chocolate bars, to be specific, in every possible flavour. They filled the air, zipping and zooming in all directions.

'AAAHHH!' Bizzy cried, dodging to avoid a toffee bar that was heading straight for her face.

This was horrible. Just as she had feared, she had turned the gala into one big mess. But Silky, Melody and Petal didn't seem angry at all, and in fact laughed delightedly as they plucked their favourite chocolate treats from the sky.

'This is so silly!' giggled Melody, as she

tumbled forwards to intercept a particularly yummy-looking chocolate-covered marshmallow bar.

'It's not supposed to be silly, it's supposed to be spectacular!' Pinx retorted, ducking away from a spear of chocolate crisp.

The crisp continued on its way to Petal, who happily grabbed it and took a giant bite.

'It *is*,' Petal noted. 'It's *spectacularly* silly.'

Silky swallowed her mouthful of malted milk bar and curled in her wings to avoid a passing buttercream.

'Exactly!' she added. 'And everyone loves it . . . except for the Angry Pixie, of course.'

They all looked down. While most of the gravity-slowed crowd was emulating the fairies and delighting in the torrents of sweets, the Angry Pixie was screaming as he flailed flat on his back.

'I'm stuck!' he shouted.

A flurry of caramel bars had crashed into

him, and the gooey insides had left him pasted to the floor.

'I demand that this party stops right now!' he wailed.

As he opened his mouth to complain again, some of the caramel dripped into it. Tasting the sweet, melting treat, the Angry Pixie paused and then grinned.

'I'm absolutely scrumptious!' he cried, and quickly stopped wailing and started licking the delicious caramel off his face.

Pinx laughed. Perhaps the party was a success after all. Bizzy, however, was still a bit upset that she hadn't been able to give everyone what they had been promised.

'Look at Cluecatcher!' Melody giggled. 'I never knew he liked chocolate bars so much.'

The fairies followed Melody's gaze. All eight of Cluecatcher's eyes were staring intently at the ceiling. As the chocolate bars whizzed his way, he spun his radar-dish ears

around and around, collecting sweets with
every turn. Then he leaned back until his huge
nostrils pointed straight to the sky and gave a
mighty sniff. . . vacuuming piles of chocolate
bars towards his face. Four of the fairies
laughed, but Silky suspected that something
other than a sweet tooth was behind
Cluecatcher's actions.

'A new Land is coming to the top of the
Tree!' Cluecatcher cried.

Immediately, Witch Whisper's voice boomed through the room.

'I am sorry, everyone, but this party is over!' she announced.

With a quick spell and a wave of her arm, she undid Bizzy's magic, banishing the flying chocolates and returning gravity to normal. As everyone started to file out, happily munching on the last of their sweets, the fairies and Witch Whisper surrounded Cluecatcher. His eyes still trained on the ceiling, Cluecatcher gave a mighty sniff. He held in the breath, rolling it around in his mouth as the fairies leaned in closer and closer, waiting with excitement to hear which land was coming to the Faraway Tree. Finally he breathed out a long, slow breath, turned to the fairies and smiled.

'Sleepover Land!' he announced.

'Sleepover Land,' Witch Whisper repeated, 'where every day is a sleepover.'

*** 14 ***

'Every day?' Bizzy asked, her eyes wide with awe.

The excitement of a new Land completely crowded out her disappointment about the party.

'Every day,' replied Witch Whisper. 'The Land's Talisman is the Bedtime Bear: the ultimate stuffed toy. Its embrace gives the gift of peaceful slumber to anyone who wishes for it. You should go now; we don't know how long the Land will be at the top of the Tree.'

'Yes! Let's go now!' Melody cried. 'I love sleepovers!'

'Then I expect you'll have an interesting time,' said Witch Whisper with a smile. 'I only hope that you remain focused and can return safely with the Talisman. And please be careful of Talon; I know you left him locked away in the Land of Giants, but he is strong and clever. If he has found a way out, he'll be after the Bedtime Bear . . . and all of you.'

The fairies promised that they would be careful and then soared out of their treehouse to the Ladder. Despite Witch Whisper's warning, they were thrilled to start their mission. After all, what could possibly be more exciting than a Land where every day is a sleepover?

Chapter Two
Sleepover Land Surprise

'I bet I'll get all kinds of ideas for new snacks in Sleepover Land,' Bizzy enthused as they climbed the Ladder. 'Sleepovers always have Stunningly Stupendous Snacks.'

'I bet they tell stories there every night,' Petal said, 'curled up in cosy sleeping bags around a campfire.'

'Oh! I should've brought my makeover kit!' Pinx cried. 'Makeovers are perfect for sleepovers!'

'I don't think we'll have time for that,' laughed Silky, 'but I do hope we have a *little* chance to look around.'

'We'll find out in just a second,' bubbled Melody. 'We're almost there!'

Sure enough, the clouds that separated the end of the Ladder from the Land were just ahead. The fairies could barely contain their excitement.

'Sleepover Land, here we come!' crowed Bizzy.

Silky, Petal, Melody and Pinx cheered happily.

'I hear something!' hissed a voice from above.

The fairies stopped in their tracks. What was that?

'Visitors!' responded another voice, and then the air was filled with sounds of shushing and stifled whispers.

'What *is* that?' wondered Pinx, her eyes narrowing.

Melody gave a sudden grin.

'I know!' she chirped. 'It sounds like someone's getting ready for a surprise party!'

'Yes!' Silky agreed, 'And we're the guests of honour!'

'Let's not spoil it,' suggested Petal. 'We'll just

fly up as if we hadn't heard anything, and when they jump out at us, we'll pretend to be completely surprised.'

'I can definitely do that!' cried Bizzy. 'I've studied every Marisolode movie, so I'm Absolutely Amazing At Acting.'

'Perfect,' said Petal. 'They'll never know we saw it coming. Let's go.'

Everyone nodded and they continued up the Ladder. The fairies pushed through the last wisps of cloud, emerged into Sleepover Land . . . and found themselves in utter darkness!

The fairies could see nothing at all, but they felt the presence of other creatures around them: their breath, the shuffling as they altered their positions, the quick bursts of more stifled giggles.

'Well!' Pinx said loudly and stiffly, trying to sound as if she had no idea that anyone wanted to surprise her. 'It is lovely to be in Sleepover Land!'

'It certainly is!' Silky added in the same stilted tone of voice. 'But it's so very, very dark!'

'Yes, it is!' Bizzy noted, following suit and speaking very loudly and carefully. 'I hope nobody jumps out to surprise us!'

Petal elbowed Bizzy in the ribs.

'What?' whispered Bizzy.

Before Petal could respond, a new voice pierced the blackness.

'NOW!' it cried.

There was a 'click' as eight circles of light appeared, each one revealing a face which was twisted into a horrible grimace: bulging eyes, tongues hanging out of mouths. The heads were attached to shadowy bodies that rustled as the figures swayed towards the fairies like zombies in the mist.

'AAAHHH!' screamed Bizzy.

The fairies backed into each other for protection, staring in horror as the eyes began

to roll and the tongues began to waggle. The fairies stumbled, bumping into one another. Suddenly a shrill voice screamed 'Get them!' The lights suddenly disappeared, leaving the terrified fairies in utter darkness. They heard a rush of footsteps.

'Ow!'

'Stop it!'

'Hey!'

The fairies cried out as their heads, faces and bodies were pummelled by blow after blow from soft, thick . . . somethings.

THWAP!

THWAP!

THWAP!

Instinctively the fairies ducked under their arms to protect their faces from the attack. Was this really Sleepover Land? What was going on?

Chapter Three

A Very Sleepee Sleepover

That's *IT*!' screamed Silky.

A burst of light exploded from her body, lighting up everything as bright as day, including their attackers. They were just eight ordinary girls!

'Ooohhh,' the girls gasped, staring at Silky's light.

Well they weren't *ordinary* girls . . . not quite. They all looked exactly alike. Each one was about six inches shorter than the fairies. They all had large, almond-shaped brown eyes, olive skin and bright blue hair, arranged in the exact same bob cut. They all wore pyjamas in the exact same shades of pink and purple with matching slippers. The only difference between the girls was the pattern on their pyjamas:

some had pinstripes, some polka dots, some a field of flowers. Even their facial expressions matched: eight dropped jaws and wide eyes as they stared at Silky. And of course, they each held a pillow – the weapons with which they had attacked the fairies.

Pinx was unimpressed.

'You've got to be kidding!' she exclaimed. 'We were all worried about *this?*'

'Did we really scare you?' asked one girl excitedly.

'We put torches under our chins,' another added. 'It's really, really creepy!'

'But why were you hitting us?' Silky demanded.

'Because it was pillow-fight time!' one girl replied.

'And now it's makeover time!' shouted another.

'You can turn off your light now,' said yet another girl to Silky. 'See?'

The girl darted to the nearest wall and
flicked a switch, illuminating every funky-
shaped, multicoloured lamp in the room. As
the lookalikes dashed off to get their
makeover kits, the fairies could see that they
were in the middle of a huge, fabulous,
playroom, filled with everything anyone could
need for a perfect sleepover. Thick, pink-and-
black zebra-striped carpets covered the floor,
with one circular section cut away to reveal a
huge ball pit, spilling over with fuchsia, white

and lime-green balls. The rest of the carpet was dotted with beanbags and sleeping bags in every colour of the rainbow. Bold orange bookshelves stood against three of the walls, their shelves filled to bursting with games, makeover kits and books.

Against the fourth wall rested a giant fluffy purple sofa, with cushions so perfectly inviting that it was almost impossible not to dive in and snuggle up. Close to the sofa was a large kitchenette with cabinets painted bright yellow with large pink polka dots. The room was clearly one of many in this odd place, since in each wall there were several doors. The only thing the room *didn't* have was a ceiling. The walls stretched up to nothing but the open air and the dim lights of the stars and moon.

Pinx was looking at the décor and smiling.

'I like this place,' she declared.

'You just like the colour scheme,' Silky

retorted, still annoyed about the pillow attack.

'Is it just me, or is there something Wildly Weird about Sleepover Land?' Bizzy asked.

'Oh no, they're very weird,' Pinx agreed.

'That's not a nice thing to say,' Melody objected. 'Maybe they're just . . . different.'

The fairies gazed at the Sleepover Land lookalikes, who were now spread across the room in groups of two, fully engrossed in doing each other's hair and makeup.

'You know what *is* weird?' Petal mused. 'I don't hear anything. No plants, no animals . . . nothing.'

That *was* weird. No matter where she went, Petal always heard some kind of background chatter from the plants and animals in the area. But while everyone considered what this might mean, Melody suddenly gasped.

'Ooh!' she exclaimed. 'I *see* an animal! Look!'

She pointed to the nearest sleeping bag,

and sure enough, there was an animal peering out of its top. It was an impossibly adorable, furry, brown animal, with black beady eyes, a leathery nose, a sewn on smile and a round belly.

'A teddy bear!' Bizzy gasped.

'*Eight* teddy bears,' Pinx elaborated, pointing to the other sleeping bags.

Now that they looked closely, the fairies could see that each one had an adorable furry brown head poking out of its top. And like the Sleepover Land girls, all the teddy bears looked exactly alike.

'Could one of them be the Talisman?' Petal asked.

But Silky was already holding up her crystal. It was perfectly clear – not even a trace of red. None of these bears was the Talisman.

'So where do we start looking?' asked Melody.

'Truth or dare time!' chorused the

Sleepover Land girls, who still all looked exactly alike . . . but now with matching newly polished nails and purple-streaked hair.

As they tucked their makeover kits away and sat in a circle for a game of truth or dare, Silky smiled at her friends. She had a plan.

'Can we play?' Silky asked.

Once again the lookalikes' jaws dropped, then quickly turned into simultaneous grins.

'Yes!' they whooped jubilantly.

Five of them raced to the fairies to take them by the hand and bring them into the circle.

'You start!' ordered a lookalike, pointing at Silky.

'Okay . . . truth or dare?' Silky asked the lookalike.

'Truth!' the lookalike proclaimed.

It seemed as if the lookalikes said or did nothing without an exclamation mark. Silky found it rather exhausting. Still, she hoped that they could help, and she was thrilled that the lookalike had chosen 'truth'. Silky leaned forwards and looked the girl in the eye.

'Do you or any of your friends know anything about a special teddy bear?' she asked.

'All sleepees' teddy bears are special!' the girl retorted.

'Sleepees?' Silky asked.

'That's what we are – sleepees!' the girl told her. 'And no sleepee goes to a sleepover without her teddy bear.'

'Because they help you sleep?' Melody asked.

All the sleepees burst into hysterical laughter, throwing their heads back at the exact same angle.

'Sleepees don't sleep, silly!' one sleepee exclaimed.

'Who sleeps at a sleepover?' another asked.

'Nobody!' chorused two more sleepees.

'Sleepovers are for fun, not sleep!'

'Yes!' the other six sleepees cheered.

'Wait,' Melody said, frowning. 'You mean . . . you *never* sleep?'

'Never!' chorused the sleepees.

'I would lose my mind if I didn't sleep,' Bizzy said, gaping at them. 'I'd be a Zany, Zonked-Out Zombie!'

Silky nodded knowingly.

'That's why they seem so odd,' she whispered to her friends. 'They're overtired and overexcited!'

'Overexcited doesn't do it justice,' Pinx whispered back. 'No sleep at all . . . that can drive someone mad!'

Several sleepees stood and pointed angrily at Silky and Pinx.

'No secrets!' they wailed.

'That's not part of the game!' another sleepee complained.

'No, it's not,' agreed the sleepee who'd been

playing with Silky, 'but we can *make* our other secret-telling friend part of the game.'

She turned to Pinx with a cold twinkle in her eye.

'Truth or dare?' she asked.

Pinx turned to Silky, who only shrugged – it was up to Pinx whether or not she wanted to play. Pinx looked at all the sleepees, who were leaning forwards expectantly.

'Fine,' Pinx sighed. 'I'll take a dare.'

A shiver of excitement ran among the sleepees.

'She chose dare!'

'It's a dare!'

'Dare!'

'She wants a dare!'

Their whispers ran back and forth, and they leaned so far towards Pinx that they nearly toppled over. Then matching smiles spread over their faces. They were not very nice smiles.

'You don't look nervous,' said the sleepee

who was leading the game. 'You should be nervous.'

'Why?' scoffed Pinx. 'It's a game. If I don't like the dare I just won't do it.'

This caused more laughter and whispers among the sleepees, and their smiles spread even wider.

'That's not how it works in Sleepover Land,' the sleepee said. 'Here, truth or dare isn't just a game. It's important. It's important to the Land itself. They say it knows if you lie in a truth or refuse a dare. And if you do, they say the Land will rise up and swallow you whole . . . and you'll never be heard from again.'

The sleepee leaned in even closer, and then opened her mouth wide and shut it again, as if swallowing someone whole. The other sleepees giggled, and soon they were all staring at Pinx and swallowing imaginary truth or dare offenders. Pinx looked at her friends.

'That's a joke, right?' she said. 'The Land itself paying attention to truth or dare? I mean . . . that's crazy.'

Silky, Petal, Bizzy, and Melody could only wince uncertainly, and gaze around them at this Land. It was a Land where everyone looked exactly alike, where no one ever slept and where it seemed that there were no plants or animals. Yes, it was absolutely crazy to think the Land itself would pay attention to a sleepover game . . . but hadn't Sleepover Land already proved to be a little bit crazy?

'So . . .' said the sleepee playing with Pinx, with an unpleasant glint in her eyes, '. . . are you ready for your dare?'

Chapter Four
The Ball Pit

If Pinx was worried, she didn't let the sleepees see it.

'I'm ready,' she said, a steely look in her eyes as she met the sleepee's gaze.

The sleepee gave a knowing smile.

'I dare you to stand up and announce to everyone in the room that we all have better fashion sense than you.'

Pinx looked as if she had been slapped. Silky was impressed despite herself: after only a few minutes together, this sleepee had found Pinx's weak point.

'No way,' Pinx declared. 'Let the Land eat me. There is no –'

'No!' Melody cut her off. 'Don't say you won't do it! What if something's listening?'

'Like the Land?' Pinx scoffed.

But Melody didn't laugh. Nor did any of the other fairies.

'We just don't know what'll happen, Pinx,' Petal told her.

'What if we can't save you?' Bizzy said.

'Or what if we can, but it takes so long that the Land moves away from the Tree?' Silky added. 'We'd be in Sleepover Land forever.'

That idea made Pinx shudder almost as much as the hideous dare. *Almost*. She looked at the grinning sleepees, who were all eager to see the consequences if she failed. She closed her eyes a moment, took a deep breath and then fixed her stare on the sleepee opposite.

'You all have better fashion sense than I do,' she muttered through fiercely gritted teeth.

The sleepees' faces fell; Pinx had succeeded. Then one sleepee brightened and turned excitedly to Petal.

'Okay – truth or dare?'

'Wait!' objected Pinx. 'Shouldn't it be my turn to ask?'

But before the sleepees could answer, one of them looked up and realised something.

'It's sunrise!' she cried.

The fairies and the sleepees immediately followed her gaze. Sure enough, the sun was just starting to peek over the top of the walls, bathing the sky in a rinse of yellow and pink. The truth or dare game was instantly abandoned as the sleepees celebrated.

'We did it!' they cried. 'We stayed up all night! Hooray!'

The elated sleepees exulted in their triumph over sleep, jumping up and down, dancing and hugging each other tightly. Tears welled in some of their eyes, so great was their pride. The fairies watched, stunned by the sleepees' manic celebrations.

'This is madness,' Petal gaped.

'I wonder what they'll do during the day,'
Melody mused.

'There are no days,' marvelled Silky,
pointing up at the sky. 'Look!'

The fairies did, and were stunned. Mere
seconds ago it had been dawn; now the sun
had raced across to the other horizon and was
about to set. The sky that moments ago had
been a sea of blue was now changing to
yellow, to red, and then quickly to a purpley-
black as darkness quickly set in once again.

The fairies weren't the only ones who
noticed the change. The sleepees cut off their
celebration to share excited looks.

'Time to switch parties!' they shouted.

Each sleepee grabbed her teddy bear and
rushed out of the room, each through a
different door. New sleepees poured through
the doors, dashing through the room on their
way to somewhere else. They were all the
same size; they all had the same brown,

almond-shaped eyes, olive skin, blue bobs and pink-and-purple pyjamas and slippers, and they were all holding identical teddy bears.

Curious, Silky flew straight up above the walls to get a better sense of what was happening. Her eyes widened.

'Girls!' she called down to the other fairies. 'You really need to see this.'

The other fairies flew up to join her.

'No way,' gasped Pinx.

'But . . . it's impossible,' added Petal.

The fairies had assumed that their playroom was part of a house in Sleepover Land. But they could now see that the *entire Land* was nothing but a series of playrooms, one after the other, as far as the eye could see. Each was decorated differently, and each had one large, unique party game. The fairies' room had the ball pit; another room housed a carousel; another contained a bouncy castle; and others held playhouses or large,

intricately decorated boxes labelled 'Funhouse' or 'Haunted House'. Each room was stocked with different games, furniture and toys . . . but they were all indoors. In fact, 'indoors' wasn't even the right word to use, because there was no *outdoors* at all. There was no soil; there were no plants or animals . . . just playrooms.

As the fairies watched from above, they could see that the whole Land was in a flurry as a seemingly endless swarm of identical sleepees darted between rooms, slamming doors. Eventually, at the same time, everyone seemed to settle in a new room. With no idea what else to do, the fairies descended back into their playroom, which was now filled with eight new sleepees. At least, the fairies assumed that they were new sleepees. They seemed to have slightly different patterns on their pyjamas than the last group of sleepees. This group was bustling in the kitchen, putting together bowls of their favourite snacks, when they heard the fairies and turned around, their mouths hanging open at the sight of their uninvited guests.

Before any of the sleepees could say anything about the fairies, one sleepee leaped up excitedly.

'Limbo Time!' she shouted.

At the sound of the call, one sleepee pulled a bright-green limbo stick from the bookcase, while another turned on limbo music.

'Hooray! Limbo!' cried the sleepees . . . and Bizzy.

Pinx turned and stared at her.

'What?' Bizzy asked. 'I Love to Limbo!'

A sleepee grabbed Bizzy's hand. '*Everybody limbos* – come on!'

She pulled Bizzy into the limbo line, and four other sleepees took hold of the other fairies.

'Please, wait,' Silky complained as she was

pushed through the limbo line. 'We're here for something very important, and we need your help.'

'LIMBO!' cried the sleepees as Bizzy successfully leaned backwards and danced under the stick.

'We don't have a lot of time,' Silky added, desperately trying to get a sleepee to listen.

'LIMBO!' cheered the sleepees, as a sleepee held Melody's hand and they both bent back

together to get under the limbo stick.

'Can somebody listen to me?' Silky shouted, frustrated.

But now it was her turn to go under the limbo stick, and the only response she got from the sleepees was an encouraging shout of, 'LIMBO!' That was it. Silky had had enough. She needed to get their attention. Summoning all her frustration, she shot a light beam at the limbo stick . . . and broke it in two. The sleepees gasped and stared at Silky in utter disbelief.

'I'm sorry,' Silky said to the sleepees. 'I didn't mean to break it. I just need you to listen for a minute. My friends and I are on a mission to save the entire Enchanted World, and we need to find a special teddy bear called the Bedtime Bear. Please, can any of you help us?'

The sleepees' eyes grew cold.

'That doesn't sound like a game!' one said.

'That's not *fun*!' another added angrily.

'Sleepovers are supposed to be fun!' wailed another sleepee.

Then one sleepee pointed at Silky.

'You're a party pooper!' she said, and then pointed at the other fairies as well. 'You're *all* party poopers!'

'PARTY POOPERS, PARTY POOPERS, PARTY POOPERS!' chanted the sleepees, dancing around the fairies.

'This is a little . . . weird,' said Melody.

'INTO THE BALL PIT!' screamed a sleepee.

Before the fairies could react, the sleepees pushed them off their feet and into the giant ball pit in the middle of the room. As the fairies toppled backwards into the giant sea of balls, the sleepees pushed a clear lid on top of the pit . . . and sat on it. From the chest down, the fairies were wedged among the colourful plastic balls.

'Hey!' cried the fairies. 'Let us out!'

They beat their fists against the lid, but they couldn't move the sleepees.

'What do we do now?' Melody asked.

'Easy,' Pinx replied. 'Silky, blast us out of here.'

'I can't,' replied Silky. 'The sleepees are sitting on the lid. I might hurt them.'

The fairies looked up through the transparent lid. The sleepees were sitting in a circle, covering the lid as they happily plaited one another's hair. They showed no sign of moving.

'I'd call to the plants and animals . . . but there aren't any,' Petal said.

'I'd try to magic a way out . . . but my wand fell into the pit and I can't reach it,' Bizzy admitted.

The fairies were silent, each of them racking their brains for a way out . . . and coming up with nothing.

'So we're just supposed to stay in here until the Land moves away from the Tree?' Pinx spluttered.

But she already knew the answer. Unless they could figure out a brilliant plan, that was *exactly* what would happen . . . and they'd be stuck in Sleepover Land forever.

Chapter Five

A Sea of Sleepees

'Ooh!' Melody exclaimed suddenly. 'I think I have an idea!'

She closed her eyes and concentrated, and within seconds she had transformed herself into ...

'Aaaah!' Pinx cried. 'Spider!'

She raised an arm to push the eight-legged creature away, but Silky grabbed her.

'Pinx, it's *Melody*.' Silky said.

'And even if it weren't, it's a living thing!' Petal added.

'Look – she's getting out!' Bizzy cried.

While the other fairies had been talking, Melody-spider had crawled her way up the wall of the pit, and was now slipping out through a crack between the ball pit lid and the floor.

'Yes!' cheered Bizzy. 'She's Spiderifically Spectacular!'

'But what is she going to do now?' Petal wondered.

The fairies stared at the spot where Melody had disappeared. Several moments passed, and nothing happened.

'I hope she's okay . . .' Silky worried.

'Especially the way some people feel about spiders,' Pinx agreed, ignoring a glare from Petal. 'I wonder what the sleepees think about –'

Her thought was interrupted by eight shrill screams of horror as the sleepees finally saw Melody.

'AAAHHH!'

'What *is* that?'

'Get it away!'

'RUN!'

Terrified, the sleepees scattered, abandoning the ball pit lid. Without the sleepees' weight on top of it, Silky, Bizzy, Petal and Pinx easily slid the lid off the pit, grabbed the edge and pulled themselves out. They were just in time. The sleepees had raced to the bookcases and grabbed boxes, dressing-up shoes and toys, and were now racing towards Melody-spider with their weapons raised high.

'STOP!' Petal screamed at the top of her lungs.

The surprised sleepees stopped in their tracks.

'Don't you dare hurt that little spider!' Petal raged.

'Spider?' asked a sleepee.

'What's a spider?' asked another.

Petal smiled. She understood life in Sleepover Land now, and had the perfect answer.

'I'd be happy to tell you all about spiders . . . for story time,' she said.

The sleepees grinned.

'It's story time!' they squealed.

In no time at all, they dropped their shoes, games and toys and raced to the big purple sofa, where they eagerly awaited Petal's tale. Petal joined them and began her tale.

'Spiders,' she told them in her gentle voice, 'are some of nature's most amazing creatures . . .'

While Petal held the attention of the sleepees, Melody-spider slipped back into the ball pit, lowering herself on a thread of silk until she found Bizzy's wand. She wrapped the wand up in layers of silk, and then dragged it behind her as she crawled back up to the edge of the pit. Then she transformed back into herself and scrambled back out, wand in hand.

'Here,' she said, handing the wand back to Bizzy.

She looked at the purple sofa, where all eight sleepees were staring at Petal with rapt attention, resting their heads in their hands as they hung on her every word.

'The sleepees really like Petal's story,' said Melody.

'While they're distracted, we should find the Talisman,' Pinx suggested.

'How?' Bizzy asked. 'There are at least a milllion sleepees, and all their teddy bears look the same. How can we find the Bedtime Bear – search every room in the Land until Silky's crystal glows?'

'Search eight teddy bears at a time?' said Silky. 'That could take forever. Unless . . .'

She flew to Petal and the other sleepees on the purple sofa.

'Excuse me,' she started, 'I hate to interrupt, but –'

'Then *don't* interrupt!' shouted a sleepee.

'Yes!' agreed another, 'You don't want to be a *party pooper*, do you?'

'No!' Silky quickly assured them. 'No party pooping, I promise. I was just thinking – you seem to like the story so much . . . maybe you want to invite some *other* sleepees to hear it too!'

The sleepees exchanged glances, and then broke into simultaneous grins.

'MEGAPARTY!' they cried.

They split up into groups of two and pushed aside the four walls of the playroom, opening them up to the four surrounding rooms.

'MEGAPARTY!' the sleepees cried to their neighbours. 'It's story time! We have a brand new story!'

'MEGAPARTY!' came return cries from the sleepees in the adjoining rooms.

The other sleepees pushed open their own walls to spread the word to the sleepees surrounding them. As the fairies watched, a dizzying number of walls were pushed open, revealing room after room of sleepees, all of whom crowded as close as they could to Petal so that they could hear the amazing new story time tale. Bizzy wrapped Silky in an enormous hug.

'You are a Genuinely Gigantic Genius!' she exclaimed. 'We don't have to go to all the sleepees; they came to us!'

'Exactly,' Silky said, looking a little bit stunned but smiling. 'I just had no idea we'd get so many.'

'And look!' Melody added. 'Your crystal!'

All the fairies looked at the crystal around Silky's neck. It was now glowing bright red.

'One of the sleepees here has the Talisman,' Pinx pronounced.

'Yes,' Silky agreed, staring out at the ocean of blue bobs, brown eyes, pink-and-purple pyjamas and teddy bears. 'But how can we tell which one?'

Chapter Six

Sleepee Selene

'I know how to find the Bedtime Bear!' Bizzy cried. 'Outside the Vault, the Talismans don't respond to magic, right? So if I can enchant all the teddy bears, the one who stays the same will be the Bedtime Bear!'

'I like that,' Pinx said. 'But how do we enchant the bears without freaking out the sleepees and making them do the party pooper thing again?'

'Same thing Petal did,' Bizzy responded. 'We make it a Perfectly Prodigious Party Pastime!'

'A *what*?' Melody asked.

But Bizzy had already taken off, flying over the group of sleepees.

'Dance time!' Bizzy shouted.

Petal was immediately forgotten as the sleepees looked up in delight.

'Hey!' Petal objected. 'I was just getting to the part about the little spider babies!'

Silky flew up to Petal and whispered in her ear that Bizzy had a plan. Petal couldn't help feeling a little disappointed about losing her audience. But she put on her best excited face.

'I mean . . . dance time!' she called out.

'Dance time!' echoed one of the sleepees. 'MEGAPARTY over!'

Bizzy's eyes widened as the sleepees turned to go back to their various rooms.

'NO!' she shouted. 'MEGAPARTY is *not* over!'

'But we have lots of Dance Times!' a sleepee objected. 'Why is this one different?'

Bizzy thought quickly.

'Because this is going to be the most amazing dance party ever, and no sleepee should miss it!' she declared. 'It'll have . . .'

Bizzy faltered as she thought about the failed Grand Galactic Gala back at the treehouse. She realised that she couldn't promise anything definite. As long as she had room for some Basic Bizzy Blunders, she'd be fine.

'I don't even *know* what it'll have – that's what makes it so exciting!' she continued. 'It'll be a Spectacularly Splashy Sleepees Surprise!'

It worked. The sleepees were entranced.

'Yes!' they squealed.

Bizzy raised her arms high, closed her eyes, and pushed every thought out of her head except 'spectacular party'. She waved her wand above her head, around, and around, and around . . . then pointed it down towards the room, all the while chanting every fun spell she could think of.

Upbeat music suddenly thrummed everywhere, impossible to resist. The floors of the various playrooms lost their carpets and

instead lit up in flashing squares of yellow, red
and white. Coloured disco balls hovered high
above the rooms, bathing them in swirling
streaks of light. Dance platforms rose into the
air, lifting surprised and excited sleepees high
above their friends. Cannons of confetti
leaned out from the folded-up walls, shooting
zillions of bits of rainbow paper into the sky.
The end result was deliriously perfect, and
Bizzy spun around amid the confetti, thrilled

beyond belief. Just a couple of things were missing.

'The music, Melody – sing!' Bizzy urged her friend.

Melody soared into the air next to Bizzy. Her voice was the perfect complement to the music, and all the sleepees cheered.

'And now . . .' Bizzy shouted to the sleepees, her eyes flashing, 'the most unique dance partners ever . . . Boogie-ing Bear Buddies!'

Pushing any clear ideas about what the bears would do out of her head, Bizzy gave her wand a mighty wave and let a spell roll off her tongue. Every teddy bear leaped out of its sleepee's arms and started dancing!

'Hurray!' the sleepees cried in excitement.

Every single sleepee jumped, shimmied and twirled with their best bear friends. Pinx shook her head in wonder at the absolutely fabulous party raging around her.

'Next treehouse party, I'm *totally* having

everyone bring a teddy bear,' she said.

'Come on,' Silky urged Pinx and Petal.
'Let's look for the Bedtime Bear while Bizzy
and Melody keep the sleepees busy.'

The three fairies spread out, flying over the
many open-walled rooms to look for a non-
dancing bear. Pinx was the one who found it,
and she cried out to Petal and Silky to join her.

Among all the dancing sleepees, one
sleepee sat in a corner all by herself. Though
she was the same size as all the other identical
sleepees, she seemed smaller somehow. Her
eyes were sad, and she sat with her knees bent
close to herself. As she watched the other
sleepees dance, she clutched her teddy bear
tightly . . . the only teddy bear in the room
that hadn't been enchanted.

As Silky, Petal and Pinx hovered over the
sleepee, Silky held up her crystal. Its red glow
had deepened. There was absolutely no doubt;
this sleepee held the Bedtime Bear.

'I'll grab the bear,' Pinx said.

But before she could dive down, Petal caught her by the elbow.

'I'm not sure that's the best idea,' said Petal.

'Why not?' Pinx demanded.

'We've seen how the sleepees react when they get upset,' Petal said. 'I think we need to handle them carefully.'

'Fine,' Pinx retorted. 'So I'll *carefully* grab the Bear.'

Pinx again started to dive down towards

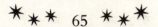

the sleepee, and again Petal grabbed her by the arm.

'Petal!' Pinx complained.

'I'm sorry!' said Petal. 'I just think that it would be better to talk to her and try to convince her to give us the bear.'

'But that could take forever!' Pinx groused.

'It could,' Silky said, 'but landing in another party pooper trap would take even longer. Petal's right: we should talk to her.'

The little sleepee didn't bat an eye as Petal floated down and sat beside her.

'Hi, there,' Petal said with a gentle smile.

'Hi,' the sleepee answered shyly.

She paused for a moment, and then turned nervously to face the fairy.

'I liked your story,' she said softly.

'Thanks,' said Petal. 'I like your pyjamas.'

Like all the sleepees' pyjamas, this girl's were purple and pink, but hers had a pattern of hearts. The girl smiled.

'Thank you,' she said.

'My name's Petal,' said Petal.

'I'm Selene,' said the sleepee.

'Why aren't you dancing, Selene?' Petal asked.

The smile vanished from Selene's face.

'No one asked me to,' she replied. 'They never do. Besides, my bear doesn't want to dance, see?'

She held out her bear to Petal, so Petal could see that it wasn't dancing. Above their heads, Pinx was going crazy, muttering, 'Grab it! Grab it!' Silky held her back.

'I see,' Petal replied, giving Selene a warm smile. 'You love your bear a lot, don't you?'

'He's my best friend,' Selene answered simply, clutching him close again. 'My only friend.'

Petal glanced up at Pinx and Silky. This was going to be hard. Silky nodded encouragingly – she knew that Petal could do this. Petal took a deep breath and then turned back to Selene.

'What if your teddy bear had the chance to do something amazing,' she said, 'like save lots and lots of creatures, all over the Enchanted World?'

Selene's eyes narrowed.

'How would he do that?' she asked.

Petal sensed that Selene was suspicious, and she decided to try a different approach. She looked up at Bizzy, who was running the dance party from above.

'That's my friend Bizzy,' Petal said. 'You saw that she can do magic, didn't you?'

'Yes,' Selene said warily.

'Well, what if Bizzy could use her magic to make you *another* friend?' said Petal. 'Or a *few* other friends. More teddy bears, maybe, or –'

Selene jumped to her feet, still clutching the bear tightly.

'You're trying to take my friend away!' she gasped.

'No!' Petal objected.

But Selene was already backing away, growing more upset by the second.

'Losing my bear wouldn't be fun at all!' she wailed. 'Sleepovers are supposed to be fun!'

'Oh, no,' groaned Pinx.

'Selene, please,' Petal entreated, but it was too late.

'You're a party pooper!' Selene wailed. 'Party pooper! Party pooper!'

'A party pooper?' cried another sleepee.

'Where?' cried another. 'Where's the party pooper?'

'PARTY POOPER!' cried several at the same time.

Within moments, every sleepee was swarming towards the sound of the initial alarm, all chanting, 'Party pooper! Party pooper! Party pooper!'

Petal knew that she should fly upwards to get away, but she couldn't give up.

'Please Selene,' she begged. 'I promise I'm not trying to hurt your feelings, but you have to understand, your bear isn't just a bear . . . *ow*!'

A mad crush of sleepees had closed in around Selene and Petal, and several of them grabbed Petal by her arms and wings as they pushed the two towards the middle of the room. High above, Melody and Bizzy flew towards Pinx and Silky in a panic.

'They've got Petal!' Melody cried. 'What do we do?'

'We help her!' Silky said. 'Come on!'

The four fairies swooped down to save their friend. At least . . . they *tried* to save their friend. Silky blasted the sleepees closest to Petal with bursts of light just strong enough to stun, but not hurt them. But with so many sleepees, the stunned ones were almost immediately replaced with new ones, just as eager to punish the party poopers, and Silky was soon grabbed into the sea of sleepees and held tight.

Melody tried turning herself into a spider again to scare the sleepees, but after Petal's charming spider stories, it no longer worked. Frustrated, she tried turning first into a snake, then into a cockroach and finally into a rat, but instead of shying away, a sleepee picked up the rat and started to squeeze. To avoid being squished, Melody had to turn back into herself.

'AAAHHH!' screeched the sleepee holding Melody. 'Scary magic! Party pooper!'

Immediately, several other sleepees grabbed Melody tightly, holding her within their swarm.

Pinx turned herself invisible and tried tickling the sleepees to move them away from Petal. It worked, but like Silky's light-beams, it only worked on one sleepee at a time, and another always stepped in to take her place. In the close crush of sleepees, Pinx's invisibility wasn't much of a defence. When the sleepees pushed up against something hard that looked like an empty space, they knew that it was Pinx, and they grabbed her.

As for Bizzy, she couldn't concentrate at all amid the crazy swarm of sleepees. Every spell she had ever known raced out of her head, and by the time she thought of anything to try, the sleepees were holding her so tightly that she couldn't move her arms to wave her wand.

The sleepees pushed the fairies and Selene into the large, candy-coloured box labelled 'Funhouse'. When they were inside, the sleepees shut the door and locked it. The screams and shouts of 'party pooper' ended, and the sleepees went back to their dance party as if nothing had happened.

Chapter Seven

The Funhouse

There were only five fairies and Selene trapped inside the Funhouse, but as the fairies looked at their new surroundings it seemed as if there were hundreds of fairies and sleepees. The walls, ceiling and floor of the Funhouse were lined with mirrors and everyone inside was reflected many times over. But these weren't normal mirrors and their reflections twisted, stretched and squashed the fairies into all sorts of different shapes and sizes. Skinny fairies stood by fat fairies, upside-down fairies stood by zigzaggy fairies. The effect was so confusing that it made the five friends dizzy. Most of them could only sit still, feeling completely bewildered. Pinx, however, was far too upset to simply sit. She leaped up

and down, bursting with rage and her
hundreds of reflections did the same, copying
her every move.

'What is *wrong* with this Land?' she yelled. 'I
don't understand these sleepees!'

Pinx turned on Selene, who was sat silently
clutching her teddy bear.

'Explain it to me, will you?' Pinx roared.
'What is the matter with you all?'

Suddenly Pinx stopped herself, and looked confused.

'Wait – what are you doing in here?' she asked. 'You're one of them. Shouldn't you be out there dancing?'

Selene shrugged.

'It's always like that for me,' she said. 'The other sleepees don't really notice me that much, so I just get pushed along by the crowd. Nothing new, really.'

Pinx just shook her head. This was so different from the way she lived her life, she didn't even know how to reply. Silky, however, wanted more information. She wasn't sure which Selene was real and which a reflection, but she turned to the nearest one, even though it happened to be upside-down.

'Selene,' Silky asked, 'why do the sleepees get so upset with party poopers? Why is it so hard to talk about anything apart from . . . fun?'

Selene (and her upside-down reflection)

looked at Silky as if she were speaking a foreign language.

'This is Sleepover Land,' she said. 'In Sleepover Land we have sleepovers. Sleepovers are supposed to be fun. Party poopers spoil our games.'

'*Games*?' Pinx exclaimed, 'This is a game? We're sealed inside a funhouse!'

'I would try to turn myself into a spider again, but there are so many reflections . . . I don't think I could find the way out,' Melody said.

'And the mirrors would bounce my light all around the room and hurt us,' Silky added.

'So once again we're trapped with no way out,' Pinx summed up. 'No offence, Selene, but I don't like your Land at all.'

Selene just shrugged. The fairies were silent. They knew that there had to be a solution . . . but what was it?

'What if . . .' Petal began slowly, thinking as she spoke, '. . . what if Bizzy turned the funhouse into something else. Something we *could* escape.'

Bizzy opened her mouth to say that this was a bad idea, but Silky beat her to it.

'Wouldn't Bizzy's spell just bounce around the mirrors like my light?' Silky asked.

'Not necessarily,' Bizzy said. 'I should be able to adjust my spell as long as I know that there are mirrors in the way.'

'Then you could do it!' Silky brightened.

'I didn't say *that* exactly –' Bizzy began.

But Pinx interrupted her.

'It's a perfect plan,' she declared. 'So what should she change the funhouse into?'

None of the fairies seemed to have an answer, and Bizzy was secretly relieved by their silence. Then Melody hopped to her feet.

'A soap bubble!' she cried. 'If we were in a soap bubble, we could pop it with our fingers and it would disappear!'

'That's perfect!' cried Silky, turning to Bizzy. 'You can do it, right?'

Bizzy stared at her four best friends, who were looking at her with eager anticipation. The last thing in the world she wanted was to let them down, but . . .

'I . . . don't know,' she stammered. 'A soap bubble is pretty specific. Maybe if I'd stayed in Fairyland and become a master magician I could do it . . .'

'If you'd stayed in Fairyland, you wouldn't *need* to do it,' Petal gently reminded her. 'You wouldn't be here with us.'

'I know,' Bizzy said. 'But still, I just . . . I don't usually do very well with precise spells. Basic Bizzy Blunders, remember?'

'I do remember,' Petal said. 'I also remember how you magicked me back to normal in the Land of Flora.'

'Fine — one Brilliant Bizzy Bonanza in a sea of Blunders,' said Bizzy in a despairing voice. 'But what about right before that, when I made mirrors instead of meteors? Or at

Princess Twilleria's Sweet Centennial when I made a rake instead of a snake? Or just before we got here, at the party in the Treehouse: were there shooting stars? No. Shooting chocolate bars. Or what about –'

'Bizzy, stop!' laughed Silky. 'All those spells turned out to be perfect! Petal *needed* you to make mirrors; the rake stopped Talon better than any snake; and everyone loved the chocolate bars!'

'Yes, I know,' Bizzy agreed, 'and that's why I usually love doing spells even if they go wrong, because sometimes the right wrong is righter than right, right?'

'Right?' Melody suggested.

'Right,' Bizzy confirmed. 'But if this goes wrong . . . what if instead of a bubble, I magic up something that *babbles*, like a giant baby who thinks we're all toys? Or what if instead of soap, I conjure a bubble made of *rope*? How would we escape that? Or what if –'

'I've got one!' Pink cried. 'Instead of soap, you could make a bubble made of *sap*! Super-sticky. We'd never get out of it.'

'*See*?' Bizzy said to the others.

Pinx and Bizzy shared a triumphant smile, and then Pinx turned to see Silky, Petal and Melody looking at her disapprovingly.

'What?' Pinx asked. 'It's a word game. It's fun.'

'Maybe you just put too much pressure on

yourself, Bizzy,' Melody suggested. 'When I had to transform into Queen Quadrille in the Land of Music, I was so nervous that I wouldn't be able to do it . . . and at first I couldn't. I had to stop worrying and relax first.'

'Melody's right,' Silky added. 'We all make mistakes when we're under pressure. I do. Sometimes when I'm too upset, I can't even make my power work. You just have to trust yourself.'

'I don't know if I can,' Bizzy admitted.

'Then trust us,' Petal suggested. 'I know you can do this.'

'I know it too,' said Melody.

'So do I,' agreed Silky. 'I'm sure of it.'

The three fairies and their reflections all looked at Pinx, who thought for a moment and then cried, '*Soup* bubble! And it would be scalding hot so we'd all get burned!'

'Pinx!' the army of Silkys, Petals and Melodys exclaimed.

'What?' Pinx repeated. 'Of course I know she can do it. I would trust Bizzy with my life.'

Pinx said it flippantly, but Bizzy was stunned.

'You would?' she asked. 'Really?'

'You don't know that?' Pinx said in surprise. 'Of course I would. Now go for it — before I find another play on the word "soap".'

Pinx's tone was brisk, but she smiled after she said it and Bizzy beamed. It was the most heartfelt compliment she had ever received from Pinx.

'Okay — I'll do it,' Bizzy said.

An inner part of her still feared that she would mess up the spell and make everything even worse for herself and her friends, but she did her best to push those thoughts away. Bizzy's friends believed in her, and Bizzy believed in her friends.

Bizzy shut her eyes.

She took a deep breath.

And she relaxed.

Then Bizzy smiled.

Waving her wand through the air with ease, she chanted, 'Bouncerella, bubblioona, soapella, slippela, sloop!'

Chapter Eight

Bizzy's Secret

Bizzy was still smiling when she opened her eyes. For perhaps the first time ever, she didn't wonder what the actual result of her spell would be.

She knew.

It was perfect.

'You did it!' screamed Silky, Pinx, Petal and Melody as Bizzy opened her eyes.

The five of them, Selene and Selene's teddy bear were floating upwards in a giant soap bubble. Through it, they could see all the other sleepees, who were enjoying their dance party and had completely forgotten about the fairies.

'So . . . who's going to pop the bubble?' Bizzy asked.

'That honour falls to you,' grinned Silky.

Bizzy smiled. With a flourish, she brandished her wand and poked it into the bubble. It burst immediately.

'Help!' cried Selene as she started to fall.

Petal and Pinx were prepared, and quickly grabbed the sleepee by the arms so that they could fly her gently to the ground.

'It's okay,' Petal told her as they landed. 'You're safe.'

'So, can we have your teddy bear now?' Pinx demanded.

'Never!' Selene cried, hugging the bear. 'I told you, he's not just a bear, he's my friend. And if you try to take him, I promise I'll call you party poopers again. I mean it, I will.'

'You can't be serious!' Pinx cried. 'We just saved your life!'

'You didn't have to,' Selene retorted. 'It's not as if it really matters. No one cares about me.'

'Great, now you're feeling sorry for yourself,' Pinx muttered. 'Well if I'm supposed to feel sorry for you too, I don't. You know what I feel? Furious!'

Selene said nothing. She simply turned away from Pinx and stared into the distance.

'Come on, Pinx,' Melody objected. 'Selene is shy.'

'So she's shy, big deal,' Pinx said. 'We're trying to save the whole Enchanted World!'

'It *is* a big deal,' Bizzy said softly, studying Selene. 'Lots of us are shy.'

'Lots of *us*?' Silky laughed. 'Bizzy, when have you ever in your life been shy?'

'I was always shy,' Bizzy said. 'When we were kids, why do you think I always tried to magic my way into the games you played with Berry? My sister had four great friends – do you remember seeing me hanging around with my own playmates?'

'No,' Melody laughed, 'you were always too busy buzzing around us!'

Bizzy raised an eyebrow and looked at

Melody, who stopped laughing as she got it.

'Because you wanted to be our friends but were too shy to ask?' Melody asked.

'Precisely,' Bizzy said, looking at Selene and sitting down beside her. 'Then one day I made a big decision. I decided not to be shy any more. It was hard, and it was scary, and it didn't always work right away . . . but it changed my life.'

Bizzy leaned closer to Selene and spoke in a gentle voice.

'You say nobody ever notices you and you don't have any friends,' she said. 'Have you ever tried to do anything to change that?'

'What do you mean?' Selene asked, not looking at Bizzy.

'I'll tell you what I learned,' Bizzy said. 'I learned that you can't wait for other people to come to you. If you want to *have* friends, you have to *be* a friend. What do the sleepees love?'

Selene was interested but confused – it seemed to her that Bizzy had asked the most obvious question in the universe.

'What do they love?' she repeated, turning to face Bizzy. 'Sleepovers . . . snacks . . . party games –'

'Yes!' Bizzy cried. 'Party games! If you want to make friends with the sleepees and get their attention, you give them a great new party game.'

'But that's crazy,' replied Selene, hugging her teddy bear. 'What if I give them a party game and they hate it? What if they laugh at me?'

'Then you'll be no worse off than you are now,' said Bizzy with a shrug, 'but at least you will have tried. And a little later you'll try something else. Besides, we'll be here to help you. All of us.'

Selene looked around at the other fairies.

'Even her?' she asked, pointing at Pinx.

'Pinx?' Bizzy said, laughing. 'Don't let her fool you. Inside, Pinx is a Perfect Pussycat.'

Selene looked around again at the fairies and then turned back to Bizzy, looking for her answer in Bizzy's kind brown eyes.

'Okay,' Selene agreed. 'I'll do it.'

Chapter Nine

Here Come the Bears

All around them, the dance party that Bizzy had begun was still in full swing. The sleepees had not noticed the funhouse turning into a bubble, popping and releasing the fairies and Selene.

Bizzy had told Selene about a great party game, and together they had come up with the best way to present it. Selene had thought that she was ready, but as she watched the other sleepees dancing and playing with their teddy bears, she trembled and shook her head.

'I don't think we should do this,' she said. 'Look at them – I don't want to be the one who interrupts this. It won't work.'

'It will,' said Bizzy. 'You can do this. Trust yourself.'

'I don't know if I can,' Selene replied.

'Then trust us,' Bizzy told her. 'Trust *me*.'

Selene thought about it for a moment . . . and then nodded. Bizzy took her hand and flew her up to the highest dance platform. With a swirl of her wand and a few magic words, Bizzy turned off all her earlier magic. The music stopped, the floors got their carpets back and the confetti machines and disco balls disappeared. As for the teddy bears, they

simply toppled over, once again nothing more than ordinary stuffed bears. Everything went back to normal except the large platform on which stood Bizzy and Selene were standing.

The sleepees were livid.

'Who stopped the party?' one shouted.

'The party was fun!' another added.

'This isn't fun at all!' another complained.

'Sleepovers are supposed to be fun!' several sleepees cried.

Bizzy could see where this was going!

'Sleepees!' she cried quickly. 'Listen to your Supremely Stupendous Sleepee Sister . . . Selene!'

Melody sang a flourish as Bizzy stepped back and ushered Selene forwards. Silky lit her up with a spotlight. A confused murmur ran through the crowd.

'Selene?'

'Who's Selene?'

'Do you know Selene?'

Selene was pale, but she caught Bizzy's eye,

and Bizzy nodded and smiled. Selene nodded back. She held her teddy bear a little tighter, cleared her throat and spoke to the crowd.

'Game Time!' she said in a weak whisper.

There was no response and Selene turned to Bizzy, looking panic stricken. Bizzy motioned for her to say it louder. Selene took a deep breath, turned back to the crowd and threw her arms in the air.

'GAME TIME!' she shouted.

'Hurray!' erupted the sea of sleepees.

Selene smiled and stood up straighter as she told them about the game that Bizzy had taught her.

'This Gargantuanly Great Game is called Musical Teddy Bears!' she announced. 'One sleepee has to put down her bear. When the music starts, everyone passes around their teddy bears until the music stops. When that happens, the sleepee left without a teddy bear is out.'

Selene searched the sleepees' faces for their approval, feeling her confidence seeping away from her.

'Um, do you . . . like that idea?' she asked nervously.

The sleepees looked at one another, and then erupted into another cry of, 'Hurray!'

Selene grinned and turned to look at the fairies.

'Go for it, Melody!' she called.

Melody began to sing a lilting tune, and the sleepees began playing Musical Teddy Bears, laughing and giggling. Selene, her teddy bear still clutched under one arm, ran the game from the top of her dance platform, declaring who was 'out' after each round. She was so happy to be part of a game at last, she couldn't wipe the happy smile from her face. Then a group of laughing sleepees called up to her.

'Selene!' one said, 'come down and play with us!'

'Yes!' added another. 'It'll be much more fun if you play too!'

'Please, Selene!' begged another. 'Come and join the game! We can all decide who's out – come and play!'

Selene was so completely stunned that she almost forgot the word 'yes'! Her new friends reached up to help her down from the platform. But before she joined them she turned back to Bizzy.

'Thanks, Bizzy,' she said, giving Bizzy a huge hug. 'I'm glad I trusted you.'

'I'm glad you trusted yourself,' said Bizzy.

Selene looked down at the teddy bear in her arms – the Bedtime Bear. She gave it a final kiss on the snout and then handed it to Bizzy.

'Here,' she said. 'If you need him, you can take him. I'm going to go play with my friends.'

Selene let the other sleepees help her down from the platform. Bizzy watched her until

Selene disappeared into the group, just one
more sleepee having fun with a sleepover
game.

'Well done,' said Silky in a gentle voice.

Bizzy turned to see Silky, Petal and Pinx
(Melody was still singing for the sleepees'
game) smiling at her, impressed.

'Now let's get out of here and get the
Talisman back to the Tree!' Pinx pleaded.

Bizzy rattled off a quick spell to conjure up

a beautiful music box that would play the Musical Teddy Bears song on its own, setting Melody free. Bizzy knew that it was time to leave, but she couldn't quite tear herself away from the sleepees. She stood on the platform looking down at the sea of identical creatures, who were playing their game with crazy energy.

'Bizzy?' asked Petal. 'Are you okay? We really need to go.'

'I know,' Bizzy replied. 'I just wish that there were something we could do for them. I mean, they all have their own stories, just like Selene, but the way they run around from game to game . . . you'd never know it. *They* might not even know it.'

'RAAAHHH!'

Bizzy's thoughts were interrupted by an ear-splitting roar of frustration, followed by the sound of a large, angry creature slamming door after door. The sleepees looked up, confused.

'What *is* that?' one of them asked.

The fairies knew the answer all too well.

'Talon!' gasped Melody.

At that moment the Troll appeared, crashing through a far door into the expanded room.

'GIVE ME THAT TALISMAN *NOW*!' he roared.

'What's a Talisman?' asked one sleepee.

'You're loud!' scolded another.

'And you sound mean! That's not fun at all!' said a third sleepee.

'Sleepovers are supposed to be fun!' another one cried.

'You're a PARTY POOPER!' several sleepees chorused. 'Party pooper!'

The sleepees swarmed towards Talon.

'The sleepees have him cornered – let's get to the Ladder and go!' cried Silky.

The five fairies rushed off, but Talon had already seen them . . . and he had also seen the Bedtime Bear tucked under Bizzy's arm.

'NO!' he roared.

Talon was too far away and too surrounded by sleepees to reach the fairies himself, but he murmured a spell in Trollish. His crystal flashed. Then the sound of pounding feet made Melody turn and look over her shoulder.

'Oh, look!' she said, completely charmed. 'The teddy bears are coming to say goodbye!'

The other fairies looked over their shoulders as well. Talon's spell had brought the sleepees' teddy bears to life, and they were racing towards the fairies. But these weren't the charmingly cuddly creatures Bizzy had created for dance time. These stuffed animals had pointed teeth and flashing, razor-sharp claws, and they growled like grizzly bears. The enchanted teddy bears raced to the top of the Ladder even faster than the fairies could fly. They blocked the way down to the Faraway

Tree, snapping their teeth and howling.

'You have got to be kidding me,' Pinx groaned. 'We finally get the Talisman, we make it past the sleepees, and we're stopped by *teddy bears*?'

'Crazy-Carnivorous Cuddlebears!' added Bizzy.

'How do we get to the Ladder with them blocking it?' asked Melody.

The space around the top of the Ladder was so narrow that the fairies always had to go single file. With the bears gathered around that opening, there was no way to avoid them.

'We push our way through,' Silky said.

She zoomed downwards and her four friends followed her towards the mass of raging teddy bears below.

Chapter Ten

The Battle for the Bear

Silky felt sure that they could push past the teddy bears. They were *teddy bears*, after all. Even if they had been enchanted with a vicious streak, they couldn't be *that* difficult to outwit. But Silky was wrong.

The bears had the furry bodies and sweet button eyes of the gentlest of night time companions, but they fought fiercely to steal the Talisman for Talon. As soon as Silky, Pinx, Petal, Bizzy and Melody flew towards them, the bears launched a fearsome attack.

'Ow!' cried Pinx, shaking her leg to throw off several bears that had gripped on with their teeth.

Thankfully, the teddies' teeth *looked* sharper than they were; they couldn't actually break the fairies' skin. Still, it wasn't a very nice feeling to have several sets of teddy bear teeth gnawing on your limbs, and it certainly made moving difficult. Pinx shook off the little beasts and sent them flying, then turned invisible. However, the bears had no bones to break, so they just threw themselves wherever they thought Pinx might be. Many thumped and thudded to the floor, but lots of others hit their mark.

'Blast these things away from us, Silky!' Pinx screamed.

'I'm trying!' Silky cried back.

Silky sent out a burst of her laser light, but the teddies did not flinch. With nothing but stuffing under their fur, they felt no pain. Blast after blast, the bears kept coming.

'Petal, can you talk to them?' Silky called.

'They're not real animals!' Petal called back, trying to wrestle a teddy bear off her head. 'They won't listen to me! What about

Melody? Can't she sing to them?'

'It's the same thing,' Melody replied.
'They're not really alive, so they won't respond
to anything I sing.'

Suddenly she had an idea.

'Maybe they'd calm down for a friend!' she
cried.

Melody closed her eyes and concentrated,
and seconds later she had become a beautiful
teddy bear. She was the same size as the
enchanted teddies, but with lighter fur and
long lashes. The teddies stopped and stared at
this lovely new creature. The Melody bear
waved her paws at them and did a pretty little
dance. The teddy bears all stood confused,
unsure of what to make of the bear in front of
them. Then the bears seemed to remember
their mission and threw themselves at Melody.
'HEY!' cried the Melody bear, hurriedly
turning herself back into a fairy. 'You bears
are supposed to be lovable!'

'Wait!' cried Bizzy. 'I have an idea!'

She lifted her wand (with great effort, seeing as there were three teddy bears clinging to it) and waved it in the air.

'Switchelloonie-Talonella-go-get-im-erooleenie!' she cried.

The teddy bears around them widened their eyes in shock, as if hypnotised. They paused, shook their heads and then grew angry once again, growling and baring their teeth. But this time, instead of lunging after the fairies, the bears ran in the other direction.

'What are they doing?' asked Pinx. 'Bizzy, what did you do?'

'I enchanted them to attack Talon instead of us!' Bizzy laughed.

Sure enough, the bewitched teddy bears were racing across the room towards the Troll. The sleepees tried to pick them up and cuddle them, only to find that they were cuddling snarling attackers, desperate to escape the sleepees' hugs and kisses and throw themselves on Talon.

Talon had been working his way across the room to get to the fairies himself, but now a heap of teddy bears threw themselves on him and pushed him back. He struggled against them, shaking off the tiny beasts as they climbed up his body and gnawed on his ankles.

Bizzy had managed to send swarms of the bears after Talon, but there were many more between them and the Ladder. Bizzy continued to place spells on more and more bears, but the Troll began to do the same thing: enchanting the bears to go after Bizzy, Silky, Petal, Melody and Pinx. The enlarged playroom had become a confused and furry battlefield.

Teddy bears hung from Talon's nose, crawled on his head and chomped on his arms and legs. Over by the Ladder, more

bears swung from Pinx's pigtails, bounced on Melody's wings, clawed their way on to Silky's dress, clung to Petal's face and got tangled in Bizzy's curls. All the while, the teddies were grabbing at the Bedtime Bear, which the fairies kept passing between them to keep the teddies confused.

The sleepees could not understand that their teddy bears were no longer the lovable friends that they had always carried with them. They kept trying to catch and cuddle the stuffed animals, which clawed and growled at them, jumping on their heads and howling.

For some bears, the constant enchantments and changing orders were too much for their cottony brains to handle. These teddies turned on one another, attacking each other in squirming balls of agitated fur and fluff. The entire scene was a whirlwind of confusion, and with so many bears running in so many different directions, it seemed as if things could only get worse.

POP!

Everyone and everything in the gigantic playroom stopped and stared as one of the teddy bears exploded into a blizzard of fur and stuffing. It was Talon who had enchanted the bear to explode, but even he seemed stunned by the actual event. As cottony fluff rained down on everyone in the room, the fairies, sleepees, teddies and Troll watched in wonder.

Talon grinned. POP! POP! POP! Bear after bear exploded into snowy fluff as Talon enchanted toy after toy. As each bear burst, sleepees would run over to the spot where their precious bears had stood just moments before looking confused at this new game.

'I truly can't believe I'm saying this,' Pinx muttered, wrestling with five of the monster teddy bears, 'but I think Talon has the right idea.'

'I was just thinking the same thing!' Silky replied.

She concentrated all her energy and aimed a jet of light at a group of bears, exploding them into cotton and fluff.

'Perfect, Silky!' cheered Bizzy. 'Watch this!'

She rattled off a spell and flung her wand towards the team of bears clinging to Petal. POP! The teddies exploded into a haze of stuffing.

'Thanks, Bizzy!' Petal called.

Then another crush of teddy bears descended on her and she went back to the wrestling match.

Thanks to the fairies and Talon, teddy bear after teddy bear exploded into fluff and the air was filled with cotton fireworks. A giddy glee seemed to fill the playroom. Even the sleepees joined in, laughing as fluff rained down gently from the sky.

At last it was over. Apart from the Bedtime Bear, who was tucked under Bizzy's arm, not a single teddy bear remained in the room. The only sign of the vicious stuffed animals was the thick layer of woollen snow that lay on the furniture and floor. For a moment, the sleepees, the fairies and Talon stayed still and caught their breath. Then Talon's eyes locked on to the Bedtime Bear.

'Down the Ladder!' cried Silky. 'Quickly!'

The fairies raced for the Ladder, but Talon's voice cut them off.

'Do it and the sleepees suffer!' he roared.

He lunged towards the sleepees, trying to catch them in his horrible hands.

'Tag time!' cried a sleepee.

'Hurray!' whooped the sleepees.

They dodged and darted away from Talon, thinking that he had started a new game. The fairies couldn't go down the Ladder and leave the sleepees were in danger.

'They think it's fun,' Petal cried. 'They don't realise Talon can enchant living things if he touches them. They don't understand they're in danger.'

'They don't have to understand,' Silky said with a glint in her eyes. 'Games are the only things they take seriously.'

'Exactly,' Bizzy agreed.

She flew into the air so that all the sleepees could see and hear her.

'It *is* tag time!' she cried, 'and Talon the Troll is It! Whatever you do, *do not* let him touch you! If you do, the game is over and you lose! *Do not* let him touch you!'

The sleepees giggled as they ducked, dodged, and darted away from Talon's grasp.

'Nice try,' snarled Talon, 'but I'm not so easy to avoid.'

He closed his eyes and wrapped his arms around himself. He muttered a string of Trollish, and the fairies exchanged uneasy looks. They had seen Talon do this before.

'He's enchanting himself,' Pinx said.

'But how?' Melody wondered. 'What is he going to do?'

Her question was soon answered. Talon's crystal flashed and a huge grin spread across his face as his arms became impossibly long and rubbery. His extraordinarily long arms wiggled and weaved around sofas, over bookcases and through ball bins. They stretched as long as the expanded playroom; there was nowhere they couldn't reach.

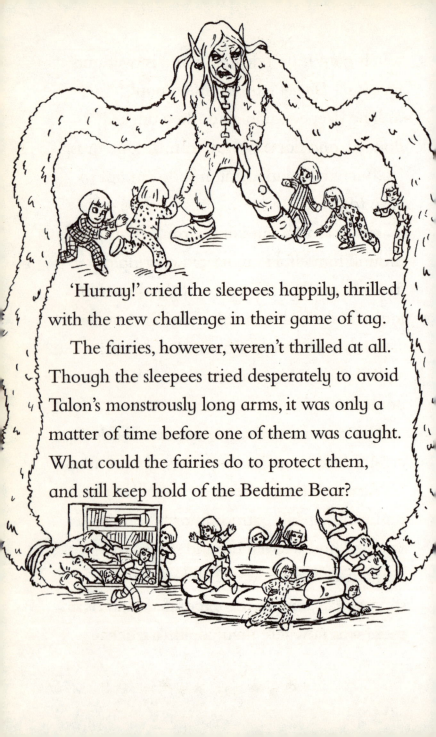

'Hurray!' cried the sleepees happily, thrilled
with the new challenge in their game of tag.

The fairies, however, weren't thrilled at all.
Though the sleepees tried desperately to avoid
Talon's monstrously long arms, it was only a
matter of time before one of them was caught.
What could the fairies do to protect them,
and still keep hold of the Bedtime Bear?

Chapter Eleven

Truth or Dare

Bizzy's head spun as she watched all the sleepees racing away from Talon's long arms. They had no idea of the horrible things that Talon might do to them if he caught them. With no sense of the danger they were in, it wouldn't be long before a sleepee let herself get caught, and Bizzy couldn't bear to think about what would happen next.

Then she had an idea.

'A Fantastical Force Field!' she cried.

'A what?' Pinx asked.

'A force field!' Bizzy explained. 'I can magic up a force field to cover all the sleepees – then Talon can't hurt them!'

She closed her eyes and concentrated, and then swooshed her wand in the air as she cried, 'Protecturellio, safellorious, forceferous!'

A stream of energy soared out of her wand and spread out over the room like a protective bubble . . . but it didn't last. Within seconds the bubble collapsed in on itself until it covered Bizzy alone.

'I can't give it enough energy,' Bizzy groaned. 'I'm not strong enough. It only covers me.'

'That's okay,' Petal assured her. 'You tried. We'll find another way to protect the sleepees.'

As Petal spoke, a sleepee barely missed getting caught by Talon's grasping fingers. Time was short, and despite Petal's words, the fairies had no way to keep the sleepees safe. Bizzy knew that she had to do something.

'Get the sleepees as far away as you can,' she told her friends. 'Take them into the other rooms. I'm going to deal with Talon myself.'

'What?' cried Melody.

'Are you crazy?' added Pinx.

'I'm not sure that's the best idea,' Petal said.

But Silky looked at Bizzy, seeing the determination on her friend's face.

'You know you can do this, don't you?' Silky asked.

Bizzy nodded.

'I trust myself,' she said simply. 'How could I not? Pinx says she'd trust me with her life.'

'I should have known you'd throw that back in my face,' Pinx grumbled. 'It doesn't mean I want you to jump into something dangerous.'

'I'll be fine,' Bizzy assured her. 'I have the force field, remember? Just get the sleepees to safety. And hold on to this.'

Bizzy gave Pinx the Bedtime Bear.

'You can do it, Bizzy,' Petal said. 'I know you can.'

'Me too,' added Melody. 'Just ... please be careful.'

Silky flew high into the air to get the sleepees' attention.

'Listen to me, sleepees!' she called. 'It's Follow-the-leader time! Quickly, follow one of us fairies, and remember, *do not let the Troll touch you!*'

'Follow-the-leader time!' several sleepees shouted.

'Hurray!' chorused several more.

Swiftly, Pinx, Silky, Petal and Melody led the sleepees in four different directions out of the expanded playroom and into four of the Land's outer rooms, where even Talon's long, rubbery arms couldn't reach them. Within seconds, the room was empty except for Bizzy and Talon. Bizzy was nervous, but she willed herself to relax and just have faith in herself.

'Hey, Talon!' she called out. 'You want to just give up, leave the sleepees alone, and let us take the Talisman down the Ladder, or would you rather face a Big Batch of Bizzy Bewitching?'

Talon laughed.

'You think you can challenge me on your own, my little wordplay fairy?' he sneered. 'You have no idea what you're up against.'

'I know *exactly* what I'm up against,' Bizzy replied. 'A bitter Troll whose magic comes from a stolen crystal.'

The Troll snarled and chanted a vicious spell in Trollish. His crystal flashed, and its light soared across the room towards Bizzy . . . only to be deflected away by her force field.

Talon roared with anger and reached out his extraordinarily long rubbery arms, but just as they were about to grab Bizzy, she recited a spell that returned them to their normal size.

Livid, Talon roared something else in Trollish. Another spell shot out of his crystal and hit Bizzy's force field, but this one didn't bounce away harmlessly. With a sharp pop the force field disappeared.

Bizzy gasped. She was sure that her friends were watching from their far-off rooms, and she guessed that they wouldn't know that her force field had been destroyed. Bizzy knew that her friends would come if she asked for their help, but she didn't want to put them in danger. Even without her force field, she felt sure that she could handle this on her own.

Talon used spell after spell to attack Bizzy. He couldn't enchant her directly, because he could only affect living things while touching them. He did, however, enchant everything else in the giant playroom: balls from the ball pit, limbo sticks, mirrors . . . he sent all these things and more flying towards Bizzy, and her mind and body whirled at super speed as she ducked, parried and blocked them with her own spells. It all happened so fast that Bizzy didn't even have time to think. If she had thought about how impossible it was to stand up against Talon's fierce attacks, she might never have been able to do it. But instead of letting herself worry about the pressure, Bizzy

just trusted herself and acted on instinct, letting the magic she had studied for so many years flow through her.

Still, it was exhausting, and part of Bizzy knew that she couldn't keep it up forever. Bizzy was a talented magician, but she was far less experienced than Talon. She needed to think of another way to defeat him . . . and quickly. Then she remembered something.

'So,' Bizzy cried out after exploding Talon's latest weapon: the purple sofa, 'we seem to be Stuck at a Startlingly Solutionless Stalemate!'

'You have put up a good fight, little fairy,' said Talon, 'but I'm not leaving without the Talisman.'

'Neither am I,' Bizzy retorted. 'But since our magic isn't getting us anywhere, and since we *are* in Sleepover Land, I propose a sleepover game: truth or dare.'

'Truth or dare?' Talon said. 'What use is that?'

'Are you saying you're afraid to play truth

or dare with me?' Bizzy challenged him.

Talon rolled his eyes.

'I'm not *afraid* of anything,' he boasted.

'Fine, we'll play. But I go first. Truth or dare?'

'Truth,' said Bizzy.

'Okay then,' Talon replied, his lips spreading into a wicked grin. 'Tell me the weakness in each of the Faraway Fairies' powers, including your own.'

Bizzy gasped – this had not been part of her plan! From their hiding places in the other rooms, Pinx, Silky, Petal and Silky gasped as well. They had learned that the Land paid attention to truth or dare, and would swallow anyone who turned down a dare or lied on a truth. Would Bizzy risk it and cover for them all, or would she tell the truth and reveal their weaknesses to their greatest enemy?

Bizzy swallowed. She took a deep breath. Then she spoke.

'Silky's light doesn't work if she's unsure of

herself, or angry with herself,' Bizzy said slowly. 'When Petal makes plants erupt out of nowhere, she becomes so weak that she must be nursed back to health with dragon-tear tea. Melody can only transform into things she knows really well, otherwise it doesn't work. Nothing can stop Pinx from turning invisible, but her biggest weakness is her pride – she believes she can do anything, even when she can't. And me . . . I almost always make mistakes with my magic. I'm getting better at controlling it, but I can't always get it exactly right. Not yet, anyway.'

'Thank you,' Talon said, grinning. 'That was most helpful. I look forward to taking advantage of it.'

Bizzy stood taller, furious that she had been forced to share her secrets, and even angrier at Talon's smug satisfaction.

'Your turn,' she snapped. 'Truth or dare?'

Talon chuckled.

'Did you really think I'd fall for the same trap I just set for you?' he asked. 'I choose dare.'

Now it was Bizzy's turn to smile.

'I dare you to disappear back to wherever you live, and stay there while my friends and I take the Talisman back to the Faraway Tree,' she said.

Talon threw back his head and laughed.

'Not a chance!' he declared.

'Do you mean that you're refusing the dare?' Bizzy asked.

'Of course I am!' Talon retorted. 'It's ridiculous!'

'Just to be clear, can you say that one more time?' Bizzy asked.

Talon rolled his eyes. Then he raised his voice and spoke very clearly in a loud voice.

'I REFUSE THE DARE!' he bellowed.

As soon as the words escaped his lips, a ghastly rumble reverberated throughout

Sleepover Land. As Talon watched in frozen horror, a giant tongue of ground ripped away its carpet cover and rose up over him, swallowing his entire body until only his head remained above ground.

Chapter Twelve

The Price of Success

Talon sputtered and fumed in his underground prison.

'Get me out of here!' he raged.

But the ground held him so tightly that he couldn't move, and even his crystal was covered in layers of dirt, leaving him completely helpless. Bizzy couldn't wipe the grin from her face.

'Hey sleepees!' she cried out, 'It's makeover time!!'

'Hurray!' cheered the sleepees.

They poured out from their hiding places, grabbed their makeover kits and swarmed around Talon, decorating his hair with gel, mousse and spray-on colour, and his face with every shade of lip gloss, blusher and eye shadow.

'Get off me this instant!' screamed Talon. 'I refuse to put up with this! Stop it immediately!'

The sleepees stood back, staring at the raging Troll in disappointment.

It's not fun at all when you shout!' chided a sleepee.

'Sleepovers are supposed to be fun!' added another.

'And that makes you a . . .'

'PARTY POOPER!' wailed the sleepees in unison.

As one ran to get her art kit, the other sleepees began the chant.

'PARTY POOPER! PARTY POOPER!'

In no time, the sleepee returned with her art kit, and grabbed her tape from inside it. While several other sleepees pressed on Talon's chin and head to keep his mouth shut, the sleepee with the tape wound it around and around Talon's head, sealing his mouth closed so that he could no longer complain.

'Hurray!' cried the sleepees when the job was done.

Then they carried on decorating Talon's face with their glosses and glitters. Silky, Petal, Pinx and Melody soared towards Bizzy and wrapped her in a giant hug.

'You did it!' Silky cheered.

But Bizzy felt ashamed. She couldn't meet the happy gazes of her friends.

'I didn't,' she admitted softly. 'I made the Biggest Bizzy Blunder ever.'

'Are you kidding?' Pinx challenged her. 'You were brilliant! Look at Talon!'

'I *thought* I was being brilliant, but look what happened,' Bizzy said. 'I told Talon everything . . .'

'You had no choice,' Petal assured her. 'If you had lied, *you'd* be the one stuck in the ground.'

'You did the right thing, Bizzy,' Melody agreed. 'Any of us would have done the same.'

Bizzy looked at her friends' reassuring faces. They were right. It had been horrible spilling all their secrets, but it had also been the only way to trap Talon, and none of them held it against her. Bizzy smiled.

'Let's get the Talisman back to the Tree,' she said.

The fairies started towards the Ladder, but Bizzy took one last look at the sleepees. As always, they were racing around with manic energy, laughing and dancing as they gave

Talon a makeover. Bizzy knew that when they grew bored of that game, they'd play another . . . and another . . . and another, never resting, never stopping, never *thinking* – never doing anything that might make them stop long enough to get tired and risk falling asleep.

'I still wish there was something we could do for them,' Bizzy said. 'I hate to think of them staying like this forever.'

'What can we do?' Melody asked. 'We can't *make* them go to sleep.'

Suddenly Silky smiled.

'*We* can't . . . but the Bedtime Bear can!' she said. 'Remember what Witch Whisper told us? It's the ultimate stuffed toy. Its hug gives the gift of peaceful slumber to anyone who asks.'

'But how do we get them to ask?' Petal asked. 'The sleepees don't think they need to sleep.'

Now it was Pinx's turn to grin as an idea came to her. She soared into the air to get the sleepees' attention.

'Game time, everybody!' she announced.

'Game time!' cried the sleepees. 'Hurray!'

'This game is called "Pinx Says",' Pinx began. 'It's simple: if I call on you, you have to do exactly what Pinx says. Got it?'

'Yes!' chorused the sleepees in excitement.

'Selene!' Silky called to their sleepee friend.

Selene happily bounced to the front of the group of sleepees, thrilled to be called first. Pinx soared down to face her, and held out the Bedtime Bear.

'Selene,' she began, 'Pinx Says . . . hug this bear, and ask for a good night's sleep.'

'But I don't want to sleep!' Selene objected. 'You never sleep at a sleepover! That's not fun!'

Before anyone could tell Pinx that 'sleepovers are supposed to be fun', she said again.

'It's fun because it's silly!' she insisted. 'You

don't want to sleep, but you say it anyway!
What could be sillier than that?'

As Selene thought about it, the fairies held
their breath. Would this work, or would they
have to avoid another party pooper swarm?
Finally, Selene smiled.

'That *is* silly!' she giggled.

She took the Bedtime Bear in her arms.

'I would like a good night's sleep,' she
wished.

Closing her eyes, Selene hugged the bear as
tight as she could.

'That was fun!' she cried.

She released the bear and handed him
back to Pinx. And then she yawned.

'I feel so . . . sleepy,' Selene said.

The walls of the expanded playroom shook
with the sound of every sleepee's gasp of horror.

Yet within moments, other sleepees were
yawning too.

Then more sleepees yawned.

And even more.

'Nothing catches quicker than a yawn,' Pinx said with a grin.

Sure enough, as the fairies looked on, one sleepee after another curled up on the soft rug and fell fast asleep.

'Perfect,' said Petal. 'When they wake up after a good night's rest, life in Sleepover Land will be brand new. They will learn that the only thing better than a sleepover is cuddling up for a nap.' Careful not to wake the sleepees, the fairies moved slowly and carefully towards the Ladder, quietly stepping back down to the Tree. Bizzy was the last to go down. Just before she disappeared, she cast one final spell, covering each sleepee with a blanket, resting each head on a pillow, and snuggling a new teddy bear into each of their arms. Perfectly satisfied now, Bizzy lowered herself down the Ladder and back home.

After they had handed the Bedtime Bear to

Witch Whisper and seen it safely returned to the Vault, the fairies gathered back in their treehouse.

'So, Bizzy,' Pinx said, 'should we get everyone back together for the Grand Galactic Gala? I bet it would go perfectly this time.'

'Thanks,' Bizzy grinned, 'but I think I've had enough of parties for a little while. You know what I'd really like to do?'

It came to all of them at the same time, and they said it in perfect unison.

'Sleep!'

The five Faraway Fairies laughed and flew up to their rooms to rest, knowing that their next adventure was just around the corner.

If you can't wait for another exciting adventure with Silky and her fairy friends, here's a sneak preview . . .

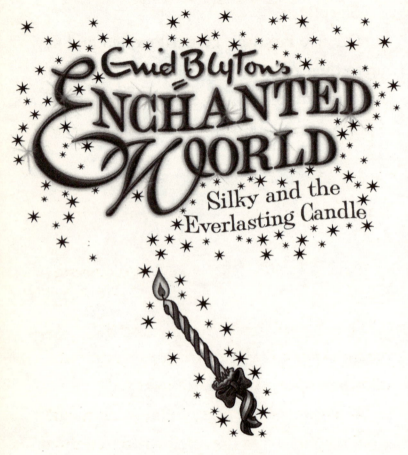

Enid Blyton's ENCHANTED WORLD

Silky and the Everlasting Candle

For fun and activities, go to
www.blyton.com/enchantedworld

Chapter One

Zuni's Surprise

'Hah!' Zuni cried triumphantly. 'I beat you again!'

The Sylvite boy was breathing heavily as he spoke but couldn't keep the grin off his face.

'Best of seven?' Silky asked, also gasping for air.

The two had been racing across the breadth of the Faraway Tree all afternoon, and were now beginning to get tired.

'What are you, a glutton for punishment?' Zuni laughed. 'I've already beaten you three times today.'

'And I beat you twice,' Silky countered. 'I'd say we're pretty evenly matched. We need four out of seven to know for sure.'

'OK then,' Zuni grinned, and he and Silky took their starting positions, both holding on to the far end of the furthest branch. 'On your marks . . . get set . . . GO!'

The two soared off across the sky . . . well at least Silky did, since she was the one with wings. Yet Zuni's lack of wings only put him at the slightest disadvantage. Zuni was an astounding athlete, and swung easily from branch to branch, turning double and triple somersaults as he weaved through the Tree. The two raced neck and neck across the vast canopy of leaves and branches; Silky ducking and zigzagging to avoid the obstacles; Zuni swinging, jumping and climbing to use it all to his advantage.

They both grinned happily as they raced; they loved the feeling of the wind rushing into their faces, and the thrill of pushing each other to their limits.

Silky and Zuni were perfectly matched and it was impossible to split them until the very last second, as Silky used her last ounce of energy to pull ahead by a whisker.

'YES!' she cried. 'I beat you! That's three to three – one more decides it all!'

'You're crazy!' Zuni panted. 'We've been up here all day. I have to get back and feed Misty.'

'What's the matter, Zuni?' Silky taunted him. 'Are you afraid you'll lose again?'

'No,' Zuni assured her. 'I'm just exhausted . . . aren't you?'

Silky was absolutely exhausted, but she couldn't tell that to Zuni.

She was up here on a mission: to distract Zuni as long as possible, so that Petal, Melody, Pinx, Bizzy, and Misty the Unicorn could decorate the treehouse and prepare it for Zuni's surprise birthday party. Then Silky was supposed to bring Zuni to the treehouse, where they had start the celebration. It was possible the other fairies were ready, but just in case they weren't . . .

'I know what it is,' Silky said playfully. 'You just get tired faster because you don't have wings.'

Silky meant it as a joke, a tease to get Zuni to race again. She certainly didn't mean to upset him. All Sylvites were athletic, but none had ever possessed the skill of Zuni, who could leap, run, dive and climb better than anyone Silky had ever seen, even in the Land of Olympians. Although he had no wings, Silky knew that Zuni was on more than equal footing with her. He had already beaten her across the canopy three times!

But Zuni didn't take Silky's comment as a joke at all. A shadow fell over his face, and he turned his dark blue eyes away from Silky.

'I can't believe you'd say that.' Zuni muttered softly.

'What?' Silky asked, stunned that her comment would have bothered Zuni in the least. Couldn't he tell she was joking? 'Zuni, I was just –'

'You know that's the reason Witch Whisper won't let me go on the Talisman missions.' Zuni snapped, cutting her off. 'I don't have wings, so she thinks I'll slow you down.'

'But Zuni, she's just being careful,' Silky replied. 'It's not because you couldn't –'

'She's not being that careful,' Zuni said bitterly. 'She's not worried about five fairies stumbling through the Enchanted World. Just me – the one who can't fly.'

Now it was Silky's turn to be affronted. '"Stumbling around the Enchanted World"? Since I've been here, I have travelled to every Land that's come to the top of the Tree, and never once have I "stumbled" anywhere. Just because I'm not a boy doesn't mean that I can't do some good in the Enchanted World.

You should know that better than anyone!'

'Forget it,' Zuni said, cutting her off. 'I'll
see you later.' And he darted off, expertly
tumbling his way back down the Tree.

'Zuni, I'm talking to you!' Silky objected,
and flew down after him, but this time Zuni
used all his acrobatic skills to quickly spin and
soar through the branches of the Tree until he
was out of sight. Furious, Silky screamed in
frustration, releasing a burst of light that flew
back up into the Tree's branches and hit the
home of Dame Washalot, who gave a startled
squeal and tipped out her bucket of dirty
washing water . . . all over Silky.

Soaked and cold, Silky suddenly realised
what a mess she had made of things. It was
Zuni's birthday. She was supposed to be
preparing him for a fabulous surprise, and
instead she had hurt his feelings, then lost her
temper. And what could she do now? Zuni
could be anywhere in the Faraway Tree, and

Silky knew him well enough to be sure that if he didn't want to be found, she'd never spot him. Abashed, she flew back to the treehouse to tell the other fairies what happened.

'SURPRISE!' cried Petal, Melody, Pinx and Bizzy when Silky opened their treehouse door.

The main room of the treehouse had been decorated beautifully in layers of multicoloured fabric and flowers in Zuni's honour. As Melody led the fairies in a spirited version of 'Happy Birthday to You', Misty the Unicorn danced through the air with a giant birthday cake balanced on her back. The top tier was made of confetti cake, and as the song ended, it exploded, raining a blizzard of candy-coloured confetti everywhere.

'What happened to you?' Pinx asked, suddenly realising that Silky was dripping dirty water all over the floor and did not have Zuni with her.

'I messed up,' Silky admitted, closing the door. But before she could say anything more, there was a knock at the door. Silky smiled hopefully. 'Maybe that's Zuni!' she said.

'Ooh! Places, everyone!' Melody whispered.

With a flourish of her wand, Bizzy returned the confetti to the top layer of the cake, which magically reconstructed itself. Quickly, Misty and the fairies soared into the corners of the room. When they were all set, Silky cried, 'Come in!'

The door opened.

Immediately, the fairies burst into song, Misty did her dance, and the cake exploded once again, raining confetti everywhere . . . confetti that landed on a rather confused Cluecatcher and Witch Whisper.

When the fairies realised who had actually entered, they gasped. The look on Cluecatcher's and Witch Whisper's face told

the fairies that there could only be one reason
for their visit.

'There's a new Land at the top of the Tree,'
Petal said knowingly, and as Cluecatcher
nodded in confirmation, the fairies gathered
round him.

'The Land of Birthdays,' Cluecatcher said
solemnly. 'Where every day is a birthday
celebration.'

'The Land of Birthdays?' Melody echoed in
delight. 'That sounds like the most wonderful
Land ever!'

'Yes . . . but that's what we said about
Sleepover Land, too,' Bizzy noted, and Melody
went quiet, remembering how strange their
last adventure had actually been.

'The Talisman for the Land of Birthdays is
the Everlasting Candle,' Witch Whisper told
the fairies. 'A birthday candle that never melts
and can neither be snuffed or blown out, no
matter how long it is lit.'

'Never be blown out! How frustrating – your wish would never come true!' Pinx turned to the other fairies. 'Promise you'll never put that candle on my birthday cake.'

'I don't think that will be a problem, Pinx,' Silky laughed. 'It's nowhere near your birthday.'

'Or any of your birthdays,' Witch Whisper added, 'which is a problem. You can't enter the Land of Birthdays unless you are accompanied by someone celebrating a birthday.'

'Then how can we possibly get up there to find the Talisman?' Petal asked.

Suddenly, the door burst open and Zuni walked into the treehouse. Eleven pairs of eyes (including Cluecatcher's four pairs) locked on Zuni immediately, but the Sylvite didn't seem to notice them. He walked straight to Silky and stood in front of her. A lock of silver hair fell over his face, and he pushed it aside so that he could meet his friend's eyes.

'I'm sorry, Silky,' he said. 'I acted horribly before, and I didn't mean any of it. You've never stumbled through anything. None of you has –'

But he stopped mid-sentence, noticing the other four fairies, Witch Whisper, Cluecatcher and Misty for the first time along with the half-exploded cake, and the confetti that still papered every surface. He also couldn't help but notice the expectant grins on everyone's faces.

'What's going on?' Zuni asked.

Silky's grin spread even wider as she took her friend's hand.

'Zuni. I believe we're about to give you the best birthday present you have ever had.'